GREEK GODS
AND
GODDESSES

By the same author and artist

Greek Myths

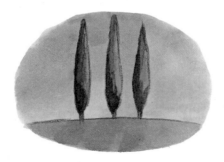

Margaret K. McElderry Books
An imprint of Simon & Schuster Children's Publishing Division
1230 Avenue of the Americas
New York, New York 10020

First published by Orchard Books, London
First United States Edition, 1998

Printed in Hong Kong
10 9 8 7 6 5 4 3 2 1

Library of Congress Catalog Card Number: 97-75538

ISBN 0-689-82084-4

GREEK GODS
AND
GODDESSES

RETOLD BY
GERALDINE MᶜCAUGHREAN

ILLUSTRATED BY
EMMA CHICHESTER CLARK

Margaret K. McElderry Books

CONTENTS

INTRODUCTION 11

TITANS AND OLYMPIANS 13
Zeus and Hera

BIG BABY 22
Hermes

PHAETON AND THE CHARIOT
OF THE SUN 30
The son of Helios

ZEUS SHINING 35
The birth of Dionysus

DIONYSUS AND THE PIRATES 40
How the dolphins began

NAMING THE CITY 47
The birth of Athena

THE IMMORTAL BLACKSMITH 54
Hephaestus and Aphrodite

CONTENTS

TWIN EAGLES   62
Artemis and Apollo

TWO LOVES OF APOLLO   71
Apollo and Hyacinthus

HALCYON DAYS   76
Halcyone and Ceyx

DEMETER AND THE PRINCELING   80
How Prince Demo almost became immortal

WHO IS THE FAIREST ONE OF ALL?   86
Hera, Athena, and Aphrodite

THE WOMAN NO ONE BELIEVED   92
Apollo and Cassandra

A FREE MAN   97
Hades and Sisyphus

THE EYES OF ARGUS   103
The birth of the peacock

A GUIDE TO THE NAMES IN GREEK MYTHOLOGY 106

For Gina and Murray
G. M.

INTRODUCTION

The Greek myths were not all written on the same day. They evolved along with Greek civilization, expanding into complex story-cycles involving more and more characters. Travelers took them to different countries, where some were altered, some reinvented. So there is no one, true version of any story, no sequence of events that can place all the gods' adventures in the "correct" order. All that is possible is to select a little from here, a little from there, for a taste of the whole.

The gods were not perfect, far from it. Their myths arise out of very "human" failings: anger, jealousy, and passion. No, the gods were not perfect, just marvelous. They atc magic food, covered astounding distances, wielded wonderful weapons, heard and answered whispered prayers, worked amazing magic.

Peopling the slopes of Mount Olympus were lesser spirits, somewhere between immortal and mortal: dryads in the trees, naiads in ponds and streams, mountain oreads; satyrs and centaurs: They ate the food of the gods, but did not live forever–only for centuries.

Of course the gods would have been nothing without mortals–chess players without chess pieces. All their excitement came from dealing with the people on Earth–loving them, hating them, helping or hounding them, marrying and abandoning them. The gods in turn were ever-present in ordinary life: their stories decorating houses and pottery or set down in plays, their sculptures gracing exquisite temples. Fortunately, such things have survived to give us a detailed picture of ancient Greece and her gods.

Here then, with the help of the Muses (who, so the Greeks say, enable us mortals to write and paint), are a few stories and pictures from Olympus, home of the gods.

TITANS AND OLYMPIANS

ZEUS AND HERA

At the very outset of everything, Heaven and Earth had twelve sons and daughters: the Titans. The youngest boy, Cronos, when his hour had come, took his father's throne by force.

Heaven cursed him: "One day your son will take power from you. Then you will taste the sorrow I taste now!"

Desperate to thwart the curse, Cronos swallowed all his own children. All, that is, but one, as yet unborn. For his pregnant wife ran away, gave birth in secret, and named the boy Zeus. Grown to manhood—finding his own hour had come—Zeus rescued his brothers and sisters from the bottomless belly of Cronos and did battle with the Titans, finally hurling them down deeper than the bottom of the universe. A few lived on, but their Age was truly past. The age of Olympians had dawned.

Zeus and his brothers shared out the world between them, drawing lots to divide up the prize.

Poseidon won the sea, realm of mermaids, whales, and reefs.

13

Hades won the Underworld, with all its gloomy caverns.

And Zeus, shining Zeus, won the Upper World: beaches and forests and streams, continents and islands, deserts and mountains.

Still, Mount Olympus was home to all three.

Next, Zeus set about peopling the Upper World. First he made a race of Gold, perfect in form and perfectly happy. They lived from the fruit on the trees and never fell ill or died.

But so easy were their days, so peaceful their nights, that they had a way of sitting down to sleep and not troubling to wake up again. So Zeus-the-Shining melted them down and left only their spirits to watch over the *next* race of people, the ones he cast from silver.

The race of Silver were beautiful and vain. They looked at themselves in the dewponds and said, "So beautiful! We must be gods!" And so they never turned their silver faces toward Mount Olympus and, in their pride, they thought the world was theirs.

So Zeus buried the race of Silver in the ground, and made the race of Bronze instead. They were no sooner born than they picked up flints and used them for tools. They made axes and spades, and began industriously to build. "This is better," said Zeus.

Then they made swords and spears and arrows and clubs, and left off building to slaughter one another. By the time their war was finished, Zeus had to begin all over again.

All that was left to him was iron. The race of Iron rusted and grew old. They worked and quarreled, loved and died. They worshiped the gods with a fearful superstition, and bombarded Olympus with their prayers. In fact, they were you. Humankind. Not much, but the best Zeus could do with base iron.

All this while, the blood of the Titan whom Zeus had overthrown lay on the dry, red, red earth. Then, up from the red, red drops, pushing their ugly faces through the soil, dragging their dragony tails behind them, came an army of giants. They tore up rocks and trees, and pelted the gods. Hard against Olympus they wrenched up Mount Ossa and balanced it on top of Mount Pelion—a ladder to reach the height of Heaven and attack the Cloudy Citadel. Their leader, Typhon, was the biggest of them all, with a hundred heads, and eyes of fire, a hundred forked black tongues in his hundred gaping mouths.

But Zeus clutched the lightning out of the sky, and thunderbolts from the glowering clouds, and he hurled them at the giants scrabbling up their mountainous siege tower. He rained on them such a hail of noise and light that Ossa and Pelion toppled and crashed, spilling them across the surface of the earth.

Only Typhon was left standing. The thunderbolts bounced harmlessly off his massive chest. The lightning he swatted away like so many fireflies, laughing. "You can't kill me, Zeus! I'm immortal like you, and like you I mean to rule the world!"

Zeus's hands were empty of weapons; he had nothing left to throw. With a hundred barbarous grins, the gigantic monster came on. "I'll rip you and I'll eat you. I'll tear you and I'll mince you. Pull the sea up over your eyes, Poseidon! Pull the earth up over your head, Hades! You don't want to see what I'm going to do to your brother!"

Then Zeus noticed Italy. It jutted out into the Mediterranean Sea like an icicle hanging from a roof. Now he bent and tore off a piece and, hurling it at Typhon with one last great roaring effort, knocked him far out to sea, creating of him a new island—Sicily. And though Typhon struggled and writhed and belched fire from his hundred mouths, his fellow giants could not come to his aid. For the Olympians were piling hills and mountains on top of *them*, burying them under a million tons of rock.

As Typhon had said, they could not die. When they writhe and struggle to break free, molten rock bursts from the mountains over them and bubbles in incandescent rivers down to the sea.

I want to marry, thought Zeus as the volcanoes simmered and their noisy

eruptions subsided. So he married Metis the Titan, and might have been happy but for something she said one night.

"You know, dear, it is prophesied that you and I will have a child as wise and great as anyone in Heaven," she said dreamily. "As mighty even as you, my love. Think of that!"

Zeus did think. "My grandfather was overthrown by my father. My father I overthrew. What if this child of hers overthrows me?"

And opening his mouth, Zeus began to yawn and stretch. The more he stretched, the wider he yawned, and by the time he settled his head on the pillow to sleep he was alone in bed. He had swallowed Metis, prophecy and all. After that, he was often troubled by headaches, but never by any regrets, for there were plenty more women in the world.

The goddess Hera heard pecking at her palace window one winter's day. She opened the shutters, and in fluttered a tiny cuckoo, shivering with cold.

"You poor little thing," said Hera, her brown eyes filling with tears. "Let me warm you." Tenderly she cradled the cuckoo against the warmth of her body and stroked its ice-speckled wings. All day she kept it with her, and at bedtime placed it on the pillow by her face.

All of a sudden, the bed groaned under a great weight, and the cuckoo disappeared. In its place, Zeus lay smiling eagerly at Hera and saying, "Kiss me, my beauty."

"Not unless you marry me!" said Hera, rolling quickly out of bed. "I've heard all about you, Zeus! I have a mind to be Queen of Heaven and the one and only love of Shining Zeus!"

So Hera married her cuckoo, and they say the mountains grew a

mattress of emerald grass and a quilt of a million flowers to make a fitting bridal bed for the King and Queen of Heaven.

But Hera told Zeus plainly: "I've heard about you and pretty women. But from this day forward your kisses are all for me, understand? Never let me hear of you wooing another woman!"

"I will never let you hear that," promised Zeus, eyes wide and innocent.

But behind his back he kept his fingers crossed.

Listen! Is that another roll of thunder? Zeus and Hera are quarreling again. It is probably about his philandering. The truth is, he simply cannot resist a pretty face. And so his life with Hera has never been peaceful.

Zeus's children are everywhere and very few of them are Hera's. He has children by mortals, children by sea nymphs, children by wood nymphs and goddesses. Hermes, messenger of the gods, has flown messages for Zeus time past number—mostly to women. Sometimes Hera tries to destroy Zeus's lovers, sometimes just to make their lives a misery. It is a kind of game—like two chess players trying to remove each other's pieces from the board. But Hera plays the game in deadly earnest.

Take for example Io.

The Princess Io wanted nothing to do with Zeus, for fear of Hera. "Leave me alone," she pleaded. "Your wife will kill me, for sure, if she thinks you care for me! Everyone knows how jealous she is!"

"She won't know," said Zeus, stroking Io's hair. And all at once, he was stroking not woman's hair but the snow-white hide of a little calf. He had turned Io into a heifer.

Hera was not fooled. She saw the flowers dripping from the calf's horns,

the way Zeus stroked that white hide and fanned away the flies. She guessed *exactly* what the calf was and, in retaliation, gave birth then and there to Argus Who Sees All.

Argus was a monster—dragonish in the length of its scaly body, but terrible for more than the rip of its claws, or its fiery breath. All over its body, large-lidded eyes glared out, watching every corner of the round world. If two eyes closed in sleep, the other ninety-eight still kept watch, unblinking. And after Argus Who Sees All coiled itself about Io, its hundred eyes scanned every horizon for a sign of Zeus, her lover.

Zeus did not dare to fight Argus. But because the task of wooing Io had been made so impossible, the thought of her grew all the sweeter. "I shall have her," he said. "I must have her. Go, Hermes, and lull this monstrous Argus to sleep with your music and your storytelling. Make it close its hundred eyes, Hermes. *Then kill it*! Do it for me, Hermes. I must have her."

That is how Hermes, messenger of the gods, came to be sitting on the ground in front of a monster and a little white calf, his lyre on his lap and his mouth full of stories.

"Greetings, Argus!"

The monster glared back with all its hundred eyes and said nothing in reply.

"You don't know much about us Olympians, do you, Argus? Being so newly born, I mean. Let me tell you a little about us. Let me tell you some of our stories."

The Argus glowered wordlessly back with the eyes on its knees, the eyes on its feet, the eyes on its shoulder and flank. But its two small ears flickered and swiveled, as though it might be listening. So Hermes began to tell stories of the gods and goddesses who live on Mount Olympus.

The sun shone agreeably warm on Argus Who Sees All, though it was too bright for some of its eyes. At the center of its coils, the little calf Io trotted unhappily to and fro, the flowers on her horns wilting in the heat. Hermes made shade for himself with a branch of laurel, and began.

Here are the stories he told.

BIG BABY

HERMES

The gods never grow old. Take Hermes. He is seventeen for all eternity, and the other gods never let him forget it. "Fetch this, Hermes. Do that, Hermes. Carry this message. Do as your half brother tells you." He even cooks for them.

But Hermes doesn't mind. He's an easygoing boy. People down on earth ask his protection when they go on journeys: Some of those wild country roads swarm with thieves and ruffians. Mind you, the thieves and ruffians ask the help of Hermes, too. They've probably heard the stories of Hermes's childhood and how light-fingered he was, even as a baby!

The day Hermes was born—in a cave in Arcadia—his mother, Maia, laid him in his cradle and kissed his tufty hair. "Don't cry now. You are a son of Zeus and a secret from his wife. If she hears you are here, Hera will hate you with a deadly hatred, and kill you if she can. So hush, my little Hermes. Don't cry." In rocking the cradle, Maia herself went to sleep.

Hermes was a big baby: big in the morning and much bigger by noon, when he clambered out of his cradle, toddled out of the cave, and met a tortoise. Banging on the tortoise's shell, he heard a throbbing hollow noise he liked. So, emptying out the tortoise, he tied threads of his mother's hair around the shell. When Maia stirred at the pulling of her hair, Hermes plucked a tune that soothed her back to sleep.

Then, slinging his newly invented lyre across his back, Hermes toddled away down the road, making up songs as he went. He was hungry. He wanted a drink of milk.

"Watch me go along,
To see what I can find.
Hear me sing my song,
With my lyre tied on behind.
I'm going to find a moo-cow
Maybe one or two cows:
I may just follow
My brother Apollo
And round up quite a few cows!"

All the way to Pieria he walked, growing all the while, and in the middle of the afternoon he found the grazing place of Apollo's shining brown cows. They were all bursting with milk, and Hermes drank all he could drink.

Then, hazel switch in hand, he began to drive the cows back the way he had come. He did not drive them headfirst, but blipped their noses, and made them walk backward, so that the tracks they left would look as if they had been coming, when in fact they had been going. He tied twigs to his feet, as well, to scuff out his own footprints.

Back along the road he toddled, singing as he went, and picking grapes off the vines at the roadside. An old woman tending the vines straightened

her aching back to watch him go by. It was a remarkable sight, after all: a baby toddling along in wicker shoes, driving a herd of back-to-front cows.

Hermes put a chubby finger to his lips, as if to say, "Don't breathe a word."

By the time he had hidden the cows—up trees, down holes, under bushes—Maia, his mother, was awake and standing at the door of the cave. "And where do you think you've been till this time of night?" she demanded, hands on hips.

Hermes climbed into his cradle: It was a bit small for him now—he had grown so much since morning. "Never you mind, Mommy," he said. Then, sucking his thumb, he quickly fell asleep.

When he woke, Apollo was standing over him, shouting till the cave echoed. "Where are my cows?"

"Agoo," said Hermes.

"You don't fool me. Where are my cows, you thieving infant!"

"A-moo?" Hermes said, and chortled.

Apollo's golden hair curled a little tighter. "An old woman saw a baby driving my cows this way. Now get out of bed. I'm taking you before the court of the gods! You can answer to Almighty Zeus for your cattle-rustling!"

***

"Silence in court!" bellowed Zeus as Hermes plucked his tortoise-lyre. "Answer the charge! Is it true, Hermes, that you stole the cattle of Apollo?"

Hermes stood up. "Almighty gods . . . gentlemen . . . ladies . . . I appeal to you—do I look like a thief? Does it seem to you probable, does it seem to you likely, that I, a little child, a mewling infant, a child of rosy innocence, should walk fifty miles on the day of my birth and carry off—like some vagabond, some deceitful rapscallion—a herd of shining cows?"

"*Yes!*" bawled Apollo.

"Silence in court!"

"And me a vegetarian! A lover of animals! The merest silken butterfly fluttering over my crib is enough to make me laugh aloud at the wondrous beauty of nature!"

"*Shyster!*" shouted Apollo.

"Silence in court!"

Hermes toddled about the courtroom, declaring his innocence, presenting his defense. He laid his baby curls on the knees of the goddesses and looked earnestly into the eyes of the gods.

He even hugged Apollo's knees, saying, "Would I steal from my own dear brother—child of my own beloved father, the mighty, the ineffable Zeus?"

Hera stood up with a scream of rage. "*Another* son of yours, Zeus?" She pointed a fearsome finger at Hermes. "For that I'll make you sorry you were ever born, baby!" Then she slammed out of the courtroom.

"You were *seen*. There are *witnesses*," snarled Apollo at his little half brother.

Hermes did not even blush, he simply took his tortoise-lyre and began to play. Apollo stared at the extraordinary instrument, overwhelmed with envy.

"I never said I didn't *take* the cows," said Hermes. "I only said I didn't *steal* the cows. The truth is, I merely *borrowed* the cows. For a drink, you know. We babies, we need our milk if we're to grow into big, strong boys. You ladies understand that, surely? Naturally, brother, you can have your cows back whenever you like. And as a token of goodwill, I'd like you to accept this lyre—I invented it yesterday."

The court cheered and clapped. Apollo snatched the lyre and began to pluck at it suspiciously. Zeus got to his feet.

"Hermes, son of Maia, you are plainly a rascal and a rogue. But you have clever fingers and a golden tongue. From this day forward, you shall be messenger of the gods . . . as soon as you have given back Apollo's shining cattle."

"Thank you, Father!" exclaimed Hermes. "Perhaps he might like these back, too." From behind his back, Big Baby Hermes produced the bow and arrow he had stolen from Apollo when he hugged him. The jury of gods gasped and stamped their feet, laughing at the outrageous audacity of the child. Even Apollo could not stay angry with a half brother who had given him the first lyre in the world. They left court together, discussing philosophy and music, poetry and politics.

"You had better watch out for Queen Hera," Apollo warned his little half

brother. "She hates you with a deadly hatred. She will never let you be messenger of the gods, no matter what Zeus says."

"Oh, no? Would you like to bet on that?" replied Hermes. "If Hera drives me off Olympus, I shall teach you how to play that lyre of mine. If I make her like me, you can give me . . . what? . . . your magic wand. Agreed?"

"Agreed!" cried Apollo. "You haven't a chance."

"Well, please excuse me now," said Baby Hermes politely, "but it's time for my morning nap." He trotted away across the marble floors of Olympus, toward the hall of the Queen of Heaven.

He went to the cradle at the foot of her bed, and smiled down at her own baby son, Ares.

"Could I ask you a very great favor?" he said.

When Hera returned to her room, she lifted her baby, swaddled in lambswool, and cradled him in her arms. She fed him, she sang to him, she

rocked him—"My, what a fine, big boy you are!"— and, plucking back the swaddling from around his head, she kissed his tufty hair.

"Agoo," said Hermes. "Guess who."

It was a risk. She has a nasty temper, the Queen of Heaven. She might have beaten his brains out then and there. But she didn't. They say a woman can't feed a baby and hate it afterward. Hera and Hermes get along well now, so long as he makes himself useful: cooking, running errands. So he won his bet with Apollo—won the magic wand, too, though he still gave Apollo music lessons. In exchange, Apollo taught his half brother how to foretell the future.

Hermes proudly displayed the magic wand for Argus to see—even offered to tell the monster's fortune. But Argus only glared back and beat one great foot on the ground, as if to say, "Another story will do."

PHAETON AND THE CHARIOT OF THE SUN

THE SON OF HELIOS

Once, the weather was always pleasant, no matter where, no matter when. Each day, as now, the sun god Helios mounted his fiery chariot and rode through the Portals of Dawn, up into the sky. Nothing deflected him from his path across the blue cosmos, though each day the route changed a little, according to season.

It was from up there that he saw the nymph Clymene and fell in love with her. They had three girls and a boy—Phaeton—and although the girls were content to help their father harness the horses to his sun chariot, Phaeton wanted more.

"May I drive, Father? May I? One day? May I, please?"

"No," said Helios. "You haven't the strength. You haven't the art. The task is mine, and too much depends on it."

But Phaeton kept on wheedling and pleading for a chance to drive the chariot, and his foolish mother joined in on his behalf. "Let him, Helios. Let him drive it. Just once. Then perhaps he'll give us some peace."

"No," said Helios.

But Phaeton was a spoiled boy and accustomed to getting his way. At last he wore out the patience of Helios.

"Drive it, then! But for my sake and your own—take care. Drive no faster than I drive, and keep to the appointed path!"

Angry at himself for giving in, Helios withdrew to a turret of dark cloud, away from his pestering family.

Laughing and teasing, Phaeton's sisters happily harnessed the horses. Nostrils flared, hoofs stamping, the horses sensed an unfamiliar weight on the running board, unfamiliar hands on the reins. And no sooner did Phaeton lay hold of his father's golden whip than he cracked it in their ears.

From standing, they leaped to a gallop, eyes rolling, teeth clenching the bit between their teeth. Dawn that day was a flash of orange on the horizon, and then it was noon.

This was thrilling, exhilarating! Phaeton gave a whoop of triumph and braced his knees against the chariot sides. Perhaps a little slower, he thought. But when he did draw back on the reins, the stallions simply reared up and tossed their heads, wrenching his arms in their sockets, burning his hands as the reins pulled through his fingers. The chariot wheels left their well-trodden track.

To left and right the chariot slewed, evaporating cloudbanks, scorching

flocks of birds. The world's soothsayers looked up and foretold miracles and catastrophes as the sun zigzagged around the sky.

Phaeton tried to take control by flogging the horses with the golden whip. "Stop, I said! Slow down! Stop!" But the stallions only panicked under the whip, ducked their heads, and plowed downward—down toward the earth.

Where the fiery blaze of the chariot passed close to the earth, its forests caught fire, and black smoke rose off waving fields of flame. Rivers turned to steam, lakes boiled, and even the shallow fringes of the sea dried to salt pans, white and peppered with dying fish.

Phaeton pulled on the reins till his fingers bled. At the last moment, the horses lifted their heads before they would crash into the earth. But now they stampeded so high into the sky that the air was too thin to breathe.

Far below, the earth was robbed of its warmth; crops died, the sea froze. Sweat streaming from the necks of Helios's horses fell in large, fluffy flakes, and rivers slowed into glaciers of ice.

The blood vessels standing proud on their sweat-dark necks, the horses plunged up and down, to and fro in a frenzy of panic. And beneath them the face of the earth was transformed forever—burned or frozen or flooded.

The animals found their habitats transformed. The bears went north, seeking coolness, the penguins went south. Monkeys fled jabbering to the jungles, and the people sought shade or warmth.

Phaeton hauled on the reins till the reins frayed through on the chariot's copper prow, and snapped.

Helios emerged from his turret of cloud, his face white as the moon. "What have you done?" he howled.

Zeus emerged from the Cloudy Citadel. "What have you done, Helios, letting a child play with your chariot? My world is in ruins, and what ruin is still to come if he isn't stopped?" From his armory of thunderbolts, Zeus took the largest.

"No! No! Not my son!" screamed Clymene.

"No! No! Not Phaeton!" cried his sisters.

Zeus glared at Helios, and the sun god bowed his head. "It is the only way," he agreed.

The thunderbolt flew with perfect aim as Phaeton clung in terror to the wildly veering chariot. It struck him on the forehead, and he fell without a cry, terribly slowly, somersaulting and wheeling through clouds, past skeins of geese, and into the blue of the sea. The broken reins were found still

gripped in his hands when his sisters carried him ashore and buried him.

Three tall slender exclamations of grief, they stood by his grave swaying and moaning. "It was our fault," they wept. "We helped to harness the horses." But it was no one's fault but Phaeton's. Too proud, too rash, too spoiled, and too stupid, he brought ruin to whole tracts of his planet, and shame to his father.

Seeing the three sisters, Zeus took pity on them and turned them into poplar trees, tall, slender, and waving. But still they wept, tears of amber welling through their tree bark in big golden drops that caught the sun.

Hermes the storyteller shaded his eyes against the glare of the sun, to see if his story had lulled the monster to sleep. But Argus Who Sees All looked back at him with every one of its hundred open eyes.

ZEUS SHINING

THE BIRTH OF DIONYSUS

Listen! Is that thunder? Zeus and Hera must be quarreling again. Once, when Hera was particularly spiteful to one of his mortal sons, Zeus hung her over a cliff with an anvil tied to her feet. But all that did was make her three spans taller and put her in a bad temper for a century. And she could always find a way of getting back at her husband.

Semele, Princess of Thebes, was so pretty that Zeus fell in love with her as easily as a pebble falls into a pond. Of course he visited her not in his own magnificent shape, but disguised as an ordinary mortal. She knew who he was, but was not silly enough to take advantage. For instance, she did not ask for magical presents, or to visit Olympus, or to live forever. Zeus loved her all the more for that.

Then Hera found out. Amazingly, she did not send monsters to imprison Semele, did not conjure sharks from the sea to devour her, did not hurl boulders at her out of Heaven's windows. No, she just went and spoke to her, as one woman to another.

"I quite understand," she said, smiling ever so sweetly.

"How could you—how could anyone resist the Almighty, the Shining Zeus. Though you've never actually *seen* Zeus in all his glory, have you? Oh, you poor little thing! Never to see the true nature of your lover! How unbearable!"

"I don't mind. Really," said Semele. But her curiosity had been aroused. What *did* he really look like, her marvelous immortal? She was expecting his baby by now: Who would the baby look like? Her or the Shining Zeus?

The very next time Zeus visited her, she asked him, "Show me yourself in your true radiance, my love! Show me the Zeus I have never seen. Show me Zeus shining!"

"No!" said Zeus. "I couldn't possibly. You are a mortal woman with mortal eyes. No! Don't ask again."

But Semele could not put it out of her mind. It gnawed on her day and night—not knowing, not being allowed to know.

"You don't love me," she told Zeus. "You don't care one fig or grape for me, if you won't let me see you shining."

"No," Zeus said, and stopped her mouth with kisses.

"You love Hera more than you love me," said Semele the next time. "*She's* seen you, but I never have. Let me. Please? Please!"

"No!" Zeus said, and went home early, slamming the door.

"I think if I don't see you, I shall die," said Semele, stroking her big stomach and crying bitterly, "and then what will become of this baby of ours?"

Whether she won him around, or whether he just lost his temper, Zeus *did* show himself to Princess Semele. He pulled on his cloak, turned around three times, and passed his hands twice over his face and hair.

A thousand shadows danced on the walls of that little Theban palace, cast by a bright profusion of lights. Then the shadows themselves were burned away—so were the walls—and the garden beyond—and the trees in the neighboring orchard. Recovering his true shape, Zeus grew to such a size

that he shattered the palace, like a phoenix hatching from its egg. And like an incandescent flame, his glory scorched everything for miles around, set it ablaze. Semele was frizzled up like a moth in a candle flame.

Tears were still wet on Zeus's cheeks when he summoned Hermes, messenger of the gods, Hermes the helper. He had something in his fist—something small and fragile: an egg, Hermes thought.

"Can you find a safe place for this, boy?" he said. "It is all that is left to me of a great love." Unfolding his fingers one by one, he showed . . . Semele's unborn baby, only half formed, only halfway to being alive.

Quickly Hermes fetched a knife and cut open Zeus's thigh. Placing the unformed child inside the wound, he stitched it shut. "You realize the child will be immortal now?" Hermes said. "Born of a god."

Zeus's tears dried. His face broke into a grin. "Oh, dear," he said. "*Won't* Queen Hera be vexed."

A few weeks later, Zeus had all but forgotten Semele. Being a god, the only pain he generally felt was a nagging headache. But today a sudden sharp cramp made him snatch at his thigh. Out from between the great sinews, out through the shining, scarred skin, Dionysus was born, god of growing things, god of the vines.

Zeus called for wine and raised a toast on Olympus's snowy peak. "To Dionysus, my immortal son!" he said.

And the rage in Hera's eyes burned as red as the embers still glowing far below among the ashes of Thebes.

Hermes the storyteller looked to see what color the eyes of Argus the monster were, and whether any of them were closed in sleep. But Argus Who Sees All peered back at him, a little bleary from the bright daylight and the music of Hermes's voice, but nonetheless watchful: watching, watching for signs of a rescue attempt.

DIONYSUS AND THE PIRATES

HOW THE DOLPHINS BEGAN

Life and soul of the party, that's how people described him. Popular? Of course he was! He was the god of wine, and wherever Dionysus was, a free drink was never far away. Like seagulls behind a fishing boat, his drunken followers screeched and swooped along behind him, singing, dancing, and falling over. In fact, he moved amid a raucous, rambling party that never ended until the last centaur, satyr, nymph, or votary had keeled over and fallen asleep.

But Dionysus was not a drunkard. He had no red nose, no rolling eyes or rubbery legs: He did not drink that much. Indeed, he was a fine-looking young man with the strong, fit body of an athlete. And for all he had been brought up by the fun-loving satyrs—they'd taught him all the songs and jokes he knew!—he also liked peace and solitude. So one day, when his hangers-on had all fallen off, as it were, and lay fast asleep in the grass, Dionysus went and stood on a jutting cliff, simply looking out to the sea. The wind billowed his purple cloak and ruffled his curling black hair.

A band of pirates saw him there, and thought at

40

once, "A slave! We can sell a strapping boy like that in Africa, for gold!"
Creeping up, all slithering quiet, with knives between their teeth, they
pounced on Dionysus and bundled him aboard their pirate dhow.

The god was intrigued. Nothing like this had ever happened to him
before.

They tried to tie him to the mast. But whether they used clove hitches or
reef knots, round turns or splices, the rope simply slipped down around
the god's ankles like wet seaweed. At last, out of curiosity, he allowed
them to tie him tight.

"Do you know who I am?" he asked.

"Don't know. Don't care," snarled the captain. "Will your father pay a
ransom or your mother give her jewels to get you back? If not, we'll take
you to Africa and sell you for a slave!"

"Oh, I wouldn't do that, if I were you," said Dionysus.

The pirates laughed hollowly. "Out here on the sea, our word is law. We
do as we like and like what we do. And if you don't—well, Mr. Slave, how
do you plan to stop us?"

Dionysus did not answer, but took in a deep, deep breath. He took in the north wind, the south, and the east. He took in the west wind and a flying fish or two. The sails drooped, and the pirate ship slowed to a standstill, rocking on the swell. The pirates licked their fingers and held them in the air. Not a breath of wind.

"We're becalmed, Captain!"

Now the pirates thought this strange, but they did not think to blame their prisoner for the sudden change in the weather. They caught some fish and they counted some loot and they drank some stolen wine.

"You like wine, do you?" said Dionysus. All the pirates laughed and drank to slavery—all except the steersman, who brought Dionysus a cup of water. The sun was very hot.

Emptying his flagon, the captain hurled it overboard.

"More wine, Captain?" Dionysus said, and whistled high and long.

The prow lifted, and the ship yawed. A tide race swelled the ripples into waves, and braided the waves into mighty combers. Then their color deepened, like a bruise, to purple, and bubbles rose silvery to the surface. So did the fish, to sing.

Not until giant waves began to break over the ship did the pirates fully grasp that the sea had turned to wine. They licked the spray off their faces; they sucked their sodden shirts; they ran to and fro with hammocks to try to catch the wine that washed over the deck. They lowered so many buckets that the ship was towed along on the raging current of wine.

"*He* did it! *He* did it!" cried the steersman. "Ask him who he is!"

"I am Dionysus, god of wine," said the prisoner. "Now take me ashore, if you please."

But the pirate captain did nothing of the sort. "You? A god? Then I'm the King of the Dryads. But a magician I can sell to the circus for more than the price of a slave. So let's see some more of your magic!"

From stem to stern, the rigging shone dark green, and began to sprout. It put on leaves, it put on shoots and twining tendrils. And climbing ropes, mast and rails, it made a whole vineyard of the ship. Pale green grapes ripened into black—so many and such heavy grapes

that the ship sank lower and lower into the running sea.

First the sailors tried to fill the holds, but when the holds were full, and still the grapes kept growing, they slashed them down in panic and threw them overboard. The juice ran into their armpits, the juice dripped into their eyes. It stuck their beards to their chests, and their feet slid from under them. But they slashed and slashed with cutlasses and knives, till the vines turned back to rope again, and the ship's rigging lay in little strands and cords around their feet.

Dionysus shook off the ropes and ran his fingers through his hair.

"Enough, your honor!" begged the steersman. "We see now the power of the gods!"

"A cod for the gods!" roared the captain. "This magician is too good for the circus. I shall keep him and grow rich! Grapes and wine? What else can you do?"

At that, Dionysus lost patience with the pirates. "I am Dionysus, god of

wine, god of growing things, Olympian son of
Zeus, immortal as the sea! I have spoken
soft and I have spoken plain. I have given
you due warning. What can I do? *See
what I can do!*"

The sky turned black. In
outstretched hands, the god caught
thunderbolts as they fell, and began to
juggle them, along with crooked blades
of lightning and members of the crew.

When he whistled this time, sea monsters
rose from the deepest sea trenches, with goggling
eyes and gaping mouths and mile-long tentacles. He stamped, and
stampeded the sea god's horses. He blew, and in blowing, borrowed the
winds of Heaven. He spun that ship like a spinning top, and the moon
came up wine-red.

Dionysus leaped to the crow's nest, where phosphorescent fire blazed in
a burning ball. And when he leaped down again, Dionysus was a lion.

"Abandon ship! Abandon ship!" yelled the
captain as the lion chased him from the tiller to
the taffrail, from the prow to the poop,
chewing his braided hair.

"Swim for your lives!" yelled the pirates
as one by one they plunged overboard,
into the heaving sea.

The sea subsided, and the sky cleared.
The lion stretched out in the sunshine, and
a breeze began to blow. The steersman was in
the crow's nest, but no one else was aboard.
Around the ship, leaping and rolling, exchanging

stuttering cries, a dozen silvery creatures swam in a turquoise sea.

"I have never seen the like, your honor," said the steersman, watching their circus tumbling. "What will you name them?"

"I think I shall call them 'dolphins,'" said Dionysus, recovering his usual shape. Then, wrapping himself in his purple cloak, he walked home across the sea.

So now dolphins cruise the world's green oceans, and patrol the navy seas. At the sight of a ship they leap for joy. At the sight of a sailor they dance on their tails. It is said that, in terrible shipwrecks, they have even rescued the crew, carried them home to shallow waters, with grins on their beaky mouths. Are they trying to earn their forgiveness, for the time they insulted a god?

NAMING THE CITY

THE BIRTH OF ATHENA

Zeus's headache got worse and worse, until one day he said, "My head is splitting!" And he was right.

A great throbbing crest swelled across the crown of his head, and when he smacked his fist against it, it split open. Out rose . . . a woman.

She was fully grown, fully dressed, fully armed. In fact, she was clad in armor, with helmet, shield, and spear. And she came into the world along a chute of light so dazzling that, for a time, no one in the courts of Heaven could move or speak or think, except to think, A new goddess has been born today.

The disc of Heaven and the disc of Earth trembled like cymbals struck together, and Helios stopped the sun chariot stock-still in the sky, to stare. The goddess's mouth was open, and a cry—a battle cry—set the fish shimmering in the sea far below.

Then the warrior woman closed her mouth, struck the pavements of Olympus three times with

47

the butt of her spear, and freed the gods from their trance, like sleepwalkers startled awake.

Her eyes were a silver gray, and when she looked at her father, Zeus knew at once how long she had lain nestled against his brain, unborn. "You are the daughter of Metis, my first wife," he said, his amazement mixed with delight. Suddenly the prophecy that Metis's child would be greater than him no longer seemed such a terrible threat to Zeus: He had always imagined a son. . . .

So Zeus did not open his mouth and swallow her, as he had swallowed her mother. He did not banish her from Heaven. In fact, from the day of her birth, she was his dearest child: Pallas Athena.

"'Dear gray eyes,' he calls her," said Poseidon, as sour and surly as ever among the drafty currents of the deep sea. "The others call her 'Mighty,' 'Champion,' 'The Warlike One,' 'Protector of Little Children!' . . . 'Goddess of the City.' Well, she won't be goddess of *my* city, and she needn't think she will!"

By "his" city, Poseidon meant the new, the marvelous city being built by King Cecrops as a lesson to the world in civilized living. In time it would be home to thousands, with a host of lovely buildings—senate houses, theaters, covered markets, and bathhouses. At present it had two rivers and the Acropolis—a hill of resplendent beauty waiting, just waiting, to be crowned with a temple.

But to which of the gods would King Cecrops dedicate his perfect city?

"It's only four miles from the sea. Of *course* it must be mine," said Poseidon, striking his trident on the floor of Heaven.

"And yet I would rather like it myself," said the gray-eyed goddess standing beside Zeus's throne.

Zeus wanted Athena to have it, but thought it best to ask King Cecrops to choose. After all, the man had taught Humankind how to worship the gods properly, so he would clearly make a wise choice. And *he* could take the blame, rather than Zeus, for offending either Poseidon or Athena. Cecrops was sent for and asked, "Which god shall be patron of your new city, and give it its name, and have their temple on the hill of the Acropolis? Shall it be Poseidon or gray-eyed Athena?"

Cecrops plucked at his lower lip and considered. He could see the barbs of Poseidon's trident twinkling, see the eagle glisten on the breastplate of Athena's armor. "I shall dedicate the city to whomsoever grants it the most useful present."

Hardly were the words spoken before Poseidon drove off full tilt in his turtleshell chariot. He split the sea asunder as he entered it, and galloped in frantic circles around the amphitheater of the Undersea, so as to set the oceans spinning. Up from his stables came his white-maned storm horses, clashing their silver hoofs, stampeding over the sea's surface with arched necks and flaring nostrils.

Choosing the very finest of his steeds, Poseidon molded its watery bulk into solid horseflesh, and led it ashore on an Aegean beach—the world's first horse of flesh and blood.

"This beast I give you, Cecrops, and all its four-footed foals forevermore. From now on, your merchants may transport their goods in horse-drawn wagons, your soldiers charge into battle on horseback, your farmers plow their fields without a pick!"

Cecrops stood and clapped. He could imagine no better present. And behind him the gods and goddesses of Olympus, ranged like the judges at a trial, were clearly just as impressed. Poseidon's city it would be.

Then, all of a sudden, Athena was standing on the crest of the hill of the Acropolis, spear in hand.

No, no. This time it was not a spear she was holding, but a little tree. As she thrust it into the ground, it grew and spread its branches—leaves the shape of a spearhead, and fruit as green and black as grapes.

"This is the olive tree," she said. "You may eat its fruit or crush it and make oil—oil to cook by, to light your houses, to flavor your meat and bread. Its leaves are soft to sleep on, its shade as cool as water at noon."

And once Cecrops had tasted the olive, he had to agree that life would never be the same again for anyone whose land contained the olive tree.

"The name of my city will be Athena," said King Cecrops, "and the temple on the Acropolis shall be the Parthenon, temple to the immortal maiden Athena!"

A rumble shook the assembly of dignitaries, which seemed to come from far beneath the earth, but which really came from Poseidon's throat. He growled the growl of a ship foundering, of a sea monster grating its teeth,

of the boulders at the bottom of the sea grinding each other to sand.

Then his hand jerked and his trident flew—and struck the hill of the Acropolis like the flank of a whale.

Out of the wound spurted saltwater—not just a spring but a fountain, a geyser, a gusher of seawater pluming into the sky then falling back on the heads of the assembled immortals. Soon the ground was muddy, the puddles joined into lakes, and the whole coastal plain disappeared beneath a flood that stretched all the way to the sea. Huge waves rolled in off the five oceans, and moved on unhindered over the Thracian Plain, submerging crops, destroying houses, drowning animals who could not reach higher ground.

Huddled together at the top of the Acropolis, their arms around each others' waists, the Olympians and King Cecrops looked out over the greatest flood in the history of their world, and wondered at the jealousy of the sea god.

"Enough! You are a sullen and peevish bully, brother!" declared Zeus, pointing his great shield at the flood and drying it up in vast twisting columns of steam. "You shall pay back the people of Athens for this wanton destruction of yours! In place of soft waves, you shall deal for a time in hard, dry stones, and in place of your cold deeps, you may labor awhile in the hot sun to earn gold as they have to do each day!"

And for sending the flood, Poseidon was made to spend seven years building the walls of a city. Not Athens. It was a citadel with a wall some sixty five feet high and sixteen feet thick of shining white stone. No weapon must breach it, no attacker scale it. It was to be the greatest fortress-city in the world.

It was to be Troy.

"Have you heard of Troy?" Hermes asked the motionless form of Argus Who Sees All. The monster writhed its gigantic body, piling coil upon coil around the little white calf, as if to say, "I *am* the walls of Troy. No weapon can breach me, no attacker climb over to steal what I guard. Least of all you."

So Hermes told another story.

THE IMMORTAL BLACKSMITH

HEPHAESTUS AND APHRODITE

"Very well!" said Hera. "If Zeus can give birth to children by himself, so can I!" And she promptly had a baby son—Hephaestus.

But Hephaestus was nothing like "dear grey eyes." He was not tall and statuesque, and no one was struck dumb by his beauty. In fact, Hephaestus was bent and buckled like a little goblin, and his baby face went purple as he howled in Hera's arms. When the other gods saw him, they laughed, and could not stop laughing, which made Hera very sorry she had given birth to him at all.

When he was a little older, Hephaestus was allowed to wait on tables in the Cloudy Citadel. But his dreadful limp and his natural clumsiness meant that he often dropped the plates or spilled the food. And then the gods and goddesses laughed till they choked, at Hephaestus the bungler, Hephaestus the clodhopper. One day, as Hephaestus hurried to fill his mother's cup, he tripped and spilled wine over her from head to foot. The assembled gods roared with laughter—but Hera grabbed her clumsy child by the left leg and hurled him out of the window of Heaven.

All day long he fell, head over heels, his screams silenced by the rush of the wind past his face. Down he fell toward the bright glass mirror of the sea, which he smashed to fragments with his ugliness. Down he plunged, where the skate rays fly and the sun's rays fade to darkness. And there the sea nymphs swam to catch him in their arms.

Down where volcanoes warmed and lit the sea, among gardens of coral, they made a home for Hephaestus, not minding his ugliness, or comparing him with anyone more beautiful. They prized him for his own lovable nature—and for his clever hands.

At the volcano furnaces the mermen taught him the arts of metalwork, forging wonderful things from the broken treasure of sunken ships. Copper and iron, gold and bronze he forged, until he was more skilled than his teachers, more masterly than any craftsman in the world.

He made lighthouses of bronze, and tripods that would walk, made magic armor that could never be pierced by sword or arrow. He made cauldrons that needed no fire to heat them, and horseshoes for the sea horses. But only when he knew he was the best blacksmith in the world did he set about making his masterpiece: a present for his mother.

He made her a chair worthy of none but a queen—and a queen of queens at that. It was an exquisite throne, of unsurpassed beauty. Its feet were lions' paws, its back like pipes of Pan surmounted by huge wings of gold. Eagle talons clasped the twin orbs that decorated the arms of the chair. When it was made, Hephaestus burnished it for twelve days before asking the messenger of the gods to take it for him to the Queen of Heaven.

Hera was entranced. "Who sent me this, Hermes?" she asked.

But Hermes had promised Hephaestus not to answer that particular question. He only winked and said, "Someone who was once very close to you."

Hera waited until all the other gods and goddesses were there, including Zeus—"See what a lovely present some *admirer* has sent to me!"—then she wriggled her bottom deep into the gleaming bronze chair seat.

The chair hugged her close. Its metal arms closed around her in a gripping embrace, and the eagle talons closed around her wrists. She gave such a shriek that snow fell in avalanches from the peaks of Olympus. But though she squirmed and tugged and struggled, there was no breaking free of the terrible chair. The gods and goddesses looked on, dumbfounded.

"*You* did this, Zeus! This is one of your jokes! One of your punishments!" Hera howled.

"No," said Zeus, trying with a length of lightning to prize open the bronze manacles. He was shocked and alarmed. An enemy had succeeded in breaching the security of the Cloudy Citadel, and he was pretty sure someone would very soon be demanding a ransom to free the Queen of Heaven.

Very soon someone did. Hephaestus, his face soot-black from the forges under the sea, came striding up the slopes of Olympus, blacksmith's hammer in his hand. He went and stood in front of the bronze throne, in front of his mother.

"You scorned me," he said, jabbing a grubby, stubby finger in her face. "You gave life to me, then you did not like what you'd made so you threw me away. Even the mothers of mortals don't do that. Even the mortal women on Earth are better mothers than you were to me! Well, I have come back for the love you owe me. And since you cannot love me as a son, I need a wife who will love me as a husband!"

"A wife? A wife, yes! Zeus, give him a wife! A wife, quickly! Do as he says. This chair is getting hot."

"I don't want just *any* wife," said Hephaestus. "I want a very particular wife."

"Who! Whooo?" The bronze beneath Hera's thighs was growing uncomfortably hot.

Hephaestus's eyes were shining. "I saw her one day as I worked at my forge. I saw her on the day she was born.. She took her life out of the sea's white foam, and a seashell carried her ashore like a fairy chariot. She was wearing nothing but a cloak of golden hair, and her lips were red as coral. That is the goddess I shall marry, I said to myself: She is the picture of love. She is Aphrodite."

"*Aphrodite?*"

Suddenly all Heaven burst out laughing. Not Hera. Not Aphrodite, but every other god and goddess held their sides and rocked with laughter at the thought. Aphrodite, goddess of love? Marry this misshapen lump of immortality?

Hephaestus did not laugh with them, but he did smile. "Love is what I lack. Love is what I most desire. So, either give me Aphrodite for my bride, Mother dear, or prepare for a long, long friendship with that magic throne of yours."

Smoke began to plume from the pipes of the lovely bronze chair back, and Hera's robe started to smoulder. What could they do? Aphrodite could screw up her heart-shaped face, purse her sweetheart mouth, stamp her pretty feet all she liked: She had to marry Hephaestus in the end.

She was not kind to him; she was not true to him. But she dared not treat him too badly, for fear her bed would eat her, her bath roast her, her chariot toss her up among the stars. And such was Hephaestus's craftsmanship, learned at the Undersea forges, that the gods came to value him, in time, as highly as the most handsome among them. He built them palaces of matchless splendor, whose turrets sometimes catch the evening sun, and make the world catch its breath. He made statues of gold that walked and talked and did as they were bid. He made thunderbolts for Zeus and arrows for the hunter-gods.

He spends little time in the Cloudy Citadel now, though, because his forges are all in the volcanoes of earth and sea. His assistants are the fallen troops of the Titan army flung down into the deepest gulches of the earth when Zeus took control of Heaven. They are hideous, each with a single eye, and filthy from their work. Still, Hephaestus finds them pleasanter company than the gods. The Cyclopes care about nothing but fire and friendship and work, and the beauty of the things they craft with their gnarled, leathery hands. When Hephaestus tells jokes, their laughter echoes around the craters and caverns. They give him their love and labor and utter devotion as the master craftsman of the world—which is more than can be said for Aphrodite.

Even so, the gods no longer snigger at the mention of Hephaestus, the immortal blacksmith. Zeus needs his thunderbolts, Artemis her arrows.

When Zeus fell in love with Princess Europa, and gave her the island of Crete for a home, he asked Hephaestus to cast a giant of brass to guard the island. Now, if any stranger tries to land, they're met by Talos, his bronze arms spread wide to hug them close to his chest. And when he has hold of them, Talos starts to glow red-hot, till the strangers fall from his grasp in a shower of ashes.

Hermes drew his sword. The monster Argus appeared to be asleep from end to end. Still, to be absolutely sure, Hermes said: "Zeus setting Talos to guard Crete was rather like Hera setting you to guard this little white calf, wasn't it?"

At once a hundred green and purple eyes flashed open, and the monster lurched up onto its haunches. Its tails swirled around Io like an unfordable river, and it bared its teeth at Hermes in a most disagreeable way. The messenger of the gods retreated and began another story.

TWIN EAGLES

ARTEMIS AND APOLLO

Zeus went to the ends of the earth to discover where its center lay. He released twin eagles—one in the east, one in the west. Naturally, the eagles flew toward each other. "Wherever they meet must be the center of the world," said Zeus, "because they are twins and alike in every way."

Artemis and Apollo were twins as well, but not so very much alike. Zeus was their father, but who was their mother? Hera? Hardly. Metis? Europa? Semele? Old loves long forgotten. No, their mother was Leto the Titan. When Hera heard Leto was expecting twins, and that Zeus was the father, she vowed those babies would never be born. "Earth spare you no space to lie down in, Leto! Time grant you no minute to give birth!"

"Oh, but, Your Majesty," protested Leto, "one of them will be Artemis! So like you! Fierce in anger, her arrows sharp—and she will *hate* men!"

"Let her be born, then," said Hera, and Leto gave birth to Artemis. "Who will the second child be?" asked Hera.

"Apollo, bright as the sun!" Leto answered, carried away with pride in her unborn son. "An archer, a sportsman, a lover as handsome as his father. . . ."

"Then the world can do without him very nicely!" snapped Hera, and she forbade anyone on earth to show Leto a friendly face or lend her a kind word. "Chase her away! Not here, not there, not anywhere shall Leto find a place to give birth to her wretched boy-child!"

Leto wept and groaned, walked and sailed from coastline to island mountaintop. But people were too afraid of Hera, and turned Leto away with spits and curses.

"I must rest! I must stop! My baby wants to be born!"

At last the people of the island of Delos took pity on her. "Rest, lady. Lie down here. Hera cannot forbid what the Fates have decreed. We will be honored to give your son a home."

So Apollo, the brother of Artemis, was born on Delos, and grew into a youth so handsome that women had only to look at him to fall in love. He spent much of his time riding in the chariot of the sun, bow and arrow in hand, looking for a place to make his home, his Athens, his shrine.

A girl called Clytie caught sight of him one day and fell so deeply in love that she could not take her eyes from his golden face and curling hair and bright, sea-blue eyes. She stood so still that her feet grew into the ground. She stood so long that her body grew as thin as a flower stalk and her face gold from the flare of the sun. The gods took pity on her and turned her into the world's first sunflower, which, even now, turns its face always toward the sun passing overhead, then lets its weary flower head fall forward and drop seeds like tears from a sun-brown face.

Artemis carried bow and arrow, like her brother. She was a huntress. It did not matter to her that she was beautiful or that Apollo was handsome: She did not want the love of any man. Her train of friends and servants were all girls, and her only interest was in chasing the deer, which she could outrun on her long, lean, brown legs.

One day a mortal hunter called Actaeon came roaming by, the ground behind him awash with fifty tumbling deerhounds, all eager for a scent. Now and then a dog would throw up its head and sniff—a rabbit or a wolf. But as yet no deer had broken cover.

Hearing the bubbling of a river, Actaeon wondered if he might catch a doe or stag unaware, drinking at the water's edge. So softly, without breaking a single twig or crushing one dry leaf, he wormed his way through the bushes to see. What he saw was more intriguing than any deer.

A group of maidens were bathing in the river. Their dresses and bows and quivers hung along the tree branches, their empty shoes all lined up, toe to heel, on the bank. They floated idly from one raft of lilies to another flowery weedbed, flicking water into each others' faces and laughing. At their center swam the hunter goddess herself, a silver crescent fastening

her hair, the sun glistening in every drop of water to roll over her brown skin. Actaeon stared, knowing he should not, but powerless to look away.

Then one of his dogs barked.

Artemis opened her eyes and saw a bush on the bank quivering. "Who's there?"

Actaeon stood up shyly. "I—I didn't mean—"

The sunlight splintered on the water like ice smashed with an ax. The peaceful scene was shattered, too, with girls screaming and scrabbling ashore, snatching down their dresses from the branches, quickly dressing. Some were still laughing.

But Artemis was not.

She struck the water with her hand—once, twice, three times. The bush quivered again, and where Actaeon had stood a second before, a big stag trembled, round-eyed with shock. At the very moment Actaeon felt the weight of antlers on his head, his heart experienced the fright of a timid wild thing trapped by hunters.

Artemis did not fire her bow, though her arrows could have felled the fastest animal. Simply to kill the man would have been too kind, as she saw it. For spying on a goddess in her bath, Artemis deemed Actaeon should be hunted down by his own hounds.

He ran—his hoofed feet lent him speed, but his hounds were hungry for the chase. They came after him slavering, barking, milling and snarling, climbing over each other's backs to lay hold on the running stag. Along the valley and through a wood of briars and brambles, thickets of sharp saplings, the terrified creature fled. His antlers rattled down twigs, his bleeding flanks left his scent strong and clear on the barks of the trees.

Fifty deerhounds bayed at his heels as he broke for the open, head back, breath too spent for prayers. He ran uphill, lungs straining, hoofs slipping, feeling the dogs' hot breath on his flicking white tail.

He would have shouted out: "Hurricane! Cyrus! Bella! It's me! Your

master!" But stags are dumb and cannot shout to save themselves.

Just as he reached the top of a hill, the dogs overtook him, jaws snapping, teeth bared. . . . And when they had finished, nothing was left of the man who had accidentally offended Artemis.

Leto was right: Here was a woman Hera could like! A woman after her own heart. Artemis and the Queen of the Gods became great friends, always exchanging gossip about some foolish thing the male gods had done.

So when one of Artemis's hunter maidens caught the eye of Zeus, Artemis rooted her out like a weed.

"Go, Callisto! Never call yourself a maiden of mine!"

"Oh, but—"

"Go! If you prefer a *man*'s company to mine!"

"Oh, I don't, I don't!"

"Run! And see what *Hera* will do to you when I tell her!"

"*No!*"

Callisto ran, as Actaeon had run—not from Artemis but to get help. She ran along riverbanks and through woods, uphill and up mountain slope toward the high home of the gods.

"Zeus! Zeus, help me! My lady Artemis knows! My lady Artemis is going to tell . . ."

Zeus heard her calling, but so did Hera. The Queen ran to the window and, peering this way and that, tried to catch sight of the loathsome nymph. Her hand rose to strike . . .

And Zeus hurled magic like a thunderbolt, so that where, a moment before, Callisto had been running, now a great brown bear ambled through the groves of Olympus, soft-furred and round with unborn cub.

Too late. Hera had seen the transformation. "Do you suppose you will save her that way?" asked Hera, spiteful with scorn. She cupped her hands around her mouth and called down to her friend. "Artemis! Oh, Artemis dear! Do you see? A *bear* is loose in your hunting ground. A dangerous *bear* is loose!"

The bear quickened its loping stride. It cast its brown eyes toward Heaven and whined softly. It ran through rivers in a burst of shining spray. It loped uphill toward the dusk-darkening sky. Behind it came Artemis the huntress, with Actaeon's hounds at her heels and her maidens, running. The bear reached the very gates of the Cloudy Citadel.

But Hera had locked them.

Callisto the bear reared up on her hind paws and turned to meet the dogs and the arrows of Artemis. Hera leaned eagerly out of the windows of Heaven, to watch the sport.

But behind her a voice said, "Do you suppose you will destroy her that way? Do you really suppose you are more powerful than Shining Zeus?"

And Zeus threw magic like sheet lightning, so that the bear Callisto leaped high into the sky, dissolving into a furry blackness outlined in stars.

Soon afterward, when the constellation of the Great Bear rose into the night sky, a smaller star group followed her—Callisto's bear-cub son. And though Artemis still shoots at mother and child, her arrows fall harmlessly back to Earth, because the Great and Little Bear are made of the night air.

From her starry park in Heaven, Callisto and Arcas have witnessed the small lives and the great events of history. The first sight they saw was a pair of twin eagles meeting in the sky, dropping down to perch on a pillar of stone. Zeus's eagles had found the center of the world.

"And who do you think made his home there? At the center of the world? Artemis's twin, of course. The handsome, the vain, the marvelous, the cruel, the mighty, the selfish Apollo. My half brother," said Hermes to the monster. Argus did not appear to be listening, but the eyes along its knobbly spine scanned the sky, in search of eagles. Argus Who Sees All was also Argus Who Hears All, and not one of Hermes's words had so far escaped its small, flickering ears. It stamped one foot as if to say, "Go on."

TWO LOVES
OF APOLLO

APOLLO AND HYACINTHUS

A god who thinks the world of himself must, of course, live at the center of the world. No matter that the spot is guarded by a dragonish snake. Apollo simply wrestled it to a standstill, rattled it till its brains coddled, coiled it up like a rope, and set it on a tripod.

"From today you are my oracle," he said, staring into the snake's bloodshot eyes. "Let the magic of this place rise through the legs of this, your three-legged throne, and speak through you of Times to Come. The whole world will come here to question you. That means the whole world will come to the Temple of Apollo, here at the world's center!"

And they did, of course. Because if there is one thing that humans crave, above food and drink and wealth and love, it is to know what Fate holds in store.

Kings and heroes come from every corner of the Mediterranean to ask the Oracle, "Will I win this war?" "Who shall I marry?" "What must I fear?" "How shall I die?"

The answers, screamed out by the Oracle in her frenzied, banshee wail, may sound senseless, but somehow the visitors always make sense of them. They make their tributes to Apollo, the god of prophecy, and some whisper that Apollo is as great as Zeus—but not if Zeus is listening.

People come to Delphi for another reason, too: for the Pythian Games, which Apollo holds there. Some whisper that the games are as splendid as those of his father, Zeus. But truly there was never anything to match the Olympian Games.

They draw the greatest sportsmen in the world—gods and demigods, heroes and princes. No slaves and no foreigners are allowed within sight or sound of the field. They run and jump and throw the javelin and the discus, wrestle and compete as though to lose was to die.

The only prize is fame and a wreath of green bay leaves—which the victor immediately tosses into a bonfire as a tribute of thanks to Zeus. And by the end of the games, that bonfire is a hill of pale blue ash higher than any man could jump.

No one has won more laurel wreaths than Apollo. Still, he had been unlucky in other ways.

Apollo had a friend—a little boy with lilac eyes and fleecy hair, called Hyacinthus. No one in Greece would argue: That boy was as beautiful as any god—the most beautiful mortal ever born, and with a nature to match. He only had to enter a room and it was as if a torch had been lit, a window opened on a warm night. Everyone loved him. Everyone wanted to have him to themselves—like a work of art bid for at auction. Everyone wanted to own Hyacinthus. But Apollo won him.

Hyacinthus thought the world of Apollo, who would take him riding in the sun's chariot and teach him how to play music and throw a discus. So Hyacinthus neglected all his other friends—including Zephyrus, the West Wind.

Zephyrus could not bear to see Apollo and the boy playing and laughing together; he howled in the hollow trees and sea caves, hissed with envy through the treetops. Then he swore that if he could not have Hyacinthus, no one else would.

Apollo took Hyacinthus to the Olympic Games; to show off to him, as usual. His javelin flew as far and fast as a speeding arrow, his discus whirled like a planet across the sky. He was magnificent. Even those who pitted themselves against him had to admit it. The muscles flexed around his legs and shoulders like golden ropes binding a lion, and his mane of hair quivered in the sun. Hyacinthus was there in the crowd, standing up on his bench, shouting for his friend, half chanting, half singing: "*Apollo is the victor of victors! A laurel crown for Apollo!*" Apollo smiled in his direction and waved. Then he bent his back, spread his arms, and began to whirl about. That discus in his hand might have been the sun itself, he put such power into the throw.

But he did not see Zephyrus. No one did. There is no seeing Zephyrus. He is just a tree tossing, a breeze in the face, a sudden sharp tug in the back of a cloak. As Apollo let fly the discus, Zephyrus blew. The breeze caught the bronze disc and carried it wildly off course. It would have carried much farther than any other—but instead it veered into the crowd and struck Hyacinthus just above the ear.

He was dead before he fell from the bench. Before he touched the ground, Apollo was there to catch him. But Hyacinthus was mortal. There was nothing Apollo could do about that.

"Oh, Zeus! Don't let his beauty be lost to the world forever!" Apollo pleaded, distracted with misery.

And Zeus threw down a handful of magic—like a farmer sowing seed. Hyacinthus no longer lay in Apollo's arms: He was gone. Instead, a little flower grew where the boy's blood had touched the grass. It was the color of his eyes, and on a warm night through an open window, its scent steals in like an unseen visitor.

No living soul can describe the sound of Apollo's sorrow that day. But Hyacinthus can. Inscribed in a deeper purple on every petal of the hyacinth are the very words of his grief, "Ai! Ai! Ai!"

HALCYON DAYS

HALCYONE AND CEYX

Zephyrus, the West Wind, paid for his unkindness (though no one guessed his part in the killing).

Zephyrus had a daughter called Halcyone—almost as lovely a girl as Hyacinthus had been a boy. Like Apollo, she, too, cared more for a mortal than for all the gods put together. She married him, too: a young sailor called Ceyx.

As Apollo wept, Zephyrus danced in a frenzy of triumph and wretchedness. For in his jealousy he had robbed Apollo but destroyed his own little friend. As he danced, he inadvertently whipped the sea into a summer storm, and crests of foam sank a dozen ships.

Ceyx was onboard one of these ships.

Zephyrus tried to comfort his daughter, but she would not be comforted. She sailed the sea in any vessel that would carry her—fishing boat, caïque, or merchantman—leaning over the rail, sweeping the sea with her fingers, searching, searching, on and on, for her drowned husband. Angrily she brushed the blinding tears from her eyes, hoping to catch sight of his purple cloak, his green shirt. She called his name so loudly and

unceasingly that her father could not make her hear any of his comforting words.

So the West Wind went to Olympus, and begged his fellow gods on bended knee: "Bring Ceyx back to life, or my daughter will die of grief!"

"You know I cannot do that," said Zeus. "Mortal man has only one short life, and then his soul belongs to Hades. That is the Law."

"I would spare his soul," said Hades, moved by the West Wind's tears. "See where it flies over the sea, toward the entrance to the Underworld? But his body is gone, so how shall he live again? It is impossible."

"*Then let me die, too!*"

It was Halcyone, standing at the gate of Heaven. Across her arms hung a sodden cloak of purple, and in her hands were scraps of a green shirt.

"Do you wish so much to be with this mortal that you would give up your immortality, child?" said Zeus.

"What is everlasting life to me, but everlasting sadness?" Halcyone replied. "Let me die!"

But Zeus did not grant her wish. Instead, he threw magic, like two handfuls of feathers, which settled gently over Halcyone and over the soul of Ceyx.

The next moment, two kingfishers darted out of the windows of Heaven—green and purple and a thousand other turquoise colors stolen from the sea. They brushed wing tips, they somersaulted, and soared through the thin air and down toward the rivers and the sea. Halcyone and Ceyx were together again, and their love made them faster on the wing than any other bird—as though even eternity was too short a time to be together.

Once a year, Halcyone builds a nest of fishbones—a nest that floats on the sea—and there she lays her eggs. For fourteen days she sits brooding on her eggs, and while she does, her father tiptoes through the world with his finger to his lips, holding back every breath of wind for fear the floating nest should be disturbed. They are his grandchildren, after all, those hatching bundles of beak and claw and feather. Every year he does it—sailors call that fortnight of dead calm the Halcyon Days—and the result is a world full of kingfishers. There goes one now!

Hermes pointed to the little green and purple bird. But Argus turned not one of its hundred eyes in the direction of the fluttering kingfisher. They were all closed.

Hermes drew his sword. It made no sound slipping out of the scabbard. He crept forward on hands and knees. From the center of the coiling monster, the little white calf blinked at him with liquid brown eyes full of desperation. Hermes raised his sword . . .

"*Cock-a-doodle-doo!*"

It was Hermes's pet cockerel. It came fussing out of the bushes, pecking up worms and ants and grit. And at the sight of its owner, it threw back its head and crowed. Every one of Argus's hundred eyes opened in a flash.

But all the monster saw was Hermes furiously bouncing his pet cockerel up and down like a rubber ball, before it escaped him and rushed away into the shrubbery again, clucking indignantly.

DEMETER AND THE PRINCELING

HOW PRINCE DEMO ALMOST BECAME IMMORTAL

There *is* someone who can grant immortality to the mortals on Earth. At least she could if she cared to. But having offered it once, she may never choose to offer it again.

Demeter loved her daughter Persephone as much as any mother ever loved a child. So when one day she called her name, and Persephone did not come, Demeter searched the world over for her lost girl.

Abandoning her work of caring for the trees and crops and flowers, Demeter ran through the world calling and crying, asking everyone she met, "Have you seen her? Have you seen my girl?" She tore her hair and rent her clothes, distracted with worry and fright. "Can you tell me? Who has stolen my darling away?" But no one could answer her, nobody knew.

Her search took her to the country of King Celeus, and there she flung herself down against the palace wall, rocking and sobbing, at a loss to know where she should look next.

"You! Beggar-woman! Are you fond of children?" It was a palace maid, calling from a window in the wall.

Demeter opened her mouth to say just what wealth of love a goddess could feel . . . but then she heard the crying of a child, and something made her keep silent.

The King had a new baby son—a pretty boy, but one of those babies who never stops crying. Queen Metanira was at her wits' end, not knowing whether he was hungry, thirsty, or in pain. Demeter took the boy in her arms, breathed magic in his face, and, at once, the boy lay quiet and smiled at her.

The Queen was overjoyed, but Demeter even more so. She was transported back to a time when Persephone had been a baby in her arms—so pretty, so sweet-smelling, so safe. When the King asked her to stay on as the Prince's nurse, Demeter found herself agreeing. And the more time she spent with Demo, the more she came to love the little mite.

Sometimes during the long nights, as she sat in his nursery beside the open window, she would hear blowing in from the darkened city the sound of women crying. And she knew (because she was a goddess and a mother)

that they, too, had lost their children. The mortals of Earth were forever losing people. Death would come, pitiless as a sword, and snatch away a grandmother, an uncle, a brother . . . a child.

"One day," she said to the sleeping princeling, "I shall find my daughter Persephone. I know she won't be dead, because she is immortal, as I am. How can you mortals bear to be parted by Death? How can your hearts bear the unbearable and not break?"

And she decided, then and there, that the world must never lose Prince Demo. Never. Though it defied the laws of Heaven, she would make him immortal!

Demeter, whose hands could raise all living plants from seed to flower, knew all the mysteries of life and death. But the magic for conferring immortality on a mortal took time. Every night she would light a fire with wood she had gathered herself. Then she would lift Demo from his cradle and lay him—gently, gently—in the magical fire. He never even stirred. After a few minutes she would return him to his crib, brushing soot off his clothes with fingers as gentle as moths' wings.

"One more sleep, and you will wake to everlasting life, my darling," she crooned as she took him one last time from his cradle. She was so intent on her magic that she did not hear the door softly open behind her. She did not see the Queen's sleep-rumpled face glance in.

When Queen Metanira saw the nurse take her baby son from his crib and lay him on a blazing fire, she let out such a scream that babies all over the city awoke and began to cry. "Murderess! Witch! You wicked, wicked woman! Help! Guard! Save my boy!"

Little Demo opened his eyes and, scenting the wood smoke, began to cry. He cried still louder as his mother snatched him by his swaddling clothes and hugged him brutally close.

Demeter sat back on her haunches and sighed. "Foolish woman! Oh, you silly, timid fool! One moment more, and I would have made your son

immortal. But you have condemned him to live and die like every other earthly creature!" So saying, she gathered up the magic fire in her arms, extinguished it with another bitter sigh, and walked out of the palace into the night, to continue her search. "I've wasted too long here!" she called over her shoulder. "My own child needs me."

And that is how a mortal *almost* became immortal. Though Prince Demo lived a long and happy life, he had to die at last, and his soul drifted down to the Underworld to join the souls of his ancestors.

There he found himself no grander than any other subject in the kingdom of Hades. But he did come to meet Demeter's missing daughter. For Hades, god of the Underworld, had snatched her away from the sunlight world and carried her off to his gloomy kingdom to brighten it with her dazzling beauty.

Though her grieving mother found her at long last, she was too late to rescue Persephone from Hades's clutches. She howled and keened and laid her long hair in the lap of Shining Zeus: "Command Hades to give me back my daughter!"

"No!" said Zeus. "My poor brother Hades needs a wife to brighten his gloomy existence. She belongs to him now."

Perhaps he thought that Demeter would give up then—that she was only a silly sentimental woman, complaining. But Demeter was more determined than he knew. "Then let the crops die in the fields and Nature wither in the bud," she said, "for until I have my daughter back, I shall not lift one finger to tend the earth!"

And as the green and blue world cankered like a rotten apple at the feet of Zeus, he was forced to give in. He decreed that Persephone should live half the year with Hades, who had stolen her away. For the rest, she could return to her mother and to the earth, to help garner the fruit and comb the feathered grasses and glean the watermeadows.

So now, on a summer's night, when a child lies tossing in a fever, the mother prays to Demeter and not to Zeus. For she knows that Demeter knows the secrets of life and death. And that she cares.

Hermes, storyteller of the gods, surveyed the monstrous Argus, still and shapeless as a mountain in the gloom of dusk. All night he told stories, but the monster's eyes continued to glimmer like the nightlights in a hundred city windows.

WHO IS THE FAIREST ONE OF ALL?

HERA, ATHENA, AND APHRODITE

The race of Gold, the race of Silver, the race of Bronze: Zeus made them, then despaired of them. The race of Iron was no different. Their crops drained the goodness from the land, their fishing plundered the sea, and their cities weighed heavy on the earth's surface. They cut down trees for firewood, and they made more noise than a pack of apes in a bucket.

So Zeus resolved to *reduce* the number of mortals on the earth. All it would take would be a single golden apple and the help of the immortals—though he told them nothing of what he was planning. He gave the golden apple to Eris, god of strife, and Eris took it to a wedding.

All the gods and goddesses were there, the naiads and nereids, the dryads, the satyrs, and the centaurs. Dionysus had brought the wine, and no one begrudged the bride and groom an eternity of happiness. They had left at home their petty rivalries, and brought instead their sweetest smiles to the wedding.

No one saw Eris take out the apple and drop it casually to the ground. But everyone saw the apple.

For the fairest, said the inscription on it.

"How kind," said Hera, smiling around her in a queenly way.

"Oh, but surely–it's meant for me," said Aphrodite, goddess of love, brushing her hair back coyly. "I mean, I presume . . ."

"You presume too much. You always did," said Athena, putting her foot on the apple so that Aphrodite should not pick it up.

"I claim the apple."

The wedding guests murmured their own opinions. Then they all began to quarrel about who was fairest.

"Zeus the Shining shall decide!" declared Hera, already thinking how best to make up her husband's mind for him.

But Zeus refused. "Judge between my wife and my daughters? Impossible! Ask a mortal to choose. He'll be impartial. And let the most handsome decide the most fair. Which *is* the handsomest youth on Earth, would you say?"

On that no one disagreed. In every alcove and bower, goddesses, nymphs, and mermaids—even the bride—sighed the name "Paris!"

Paris was the Prince of Troy—an alarmingly good-looking boy who had not yet fallen in love. Hermes, messenger of the gods, was sent to fetch him. One moment he was alone, fishing on the seashore, the next he was blinking at the brightness of the Cloudy Citadel. Before him sat the three most powerful goddesses in the world, carefully arranging the drapery of their gowns. "Look, don't touch," Hermes whispered in his ear. "And above all, Paris, listen. It may be to your advantage."

As Paris passed in front of Hera's throne with its golden eagles, she bared her teeth in a smile and whispered, "Decide in my favor and I shall make you the ruler of empires."

"Thank you," said Paris. "How kind."

As he passed in front of Athena, she struck the pavement of Heaven with the butt of her spear so loudly that Paris started. "I see it now," she whispered, glaring at him with her solemn gray eyes. "I, goddess of battle, see the crown of a dozen glorious victories around your brow! What battles won't I win for the man who proclaims me fairest of all!"

"Thank you," Paris said, and gave her such a dazzling smile that she dropped her helmet.

By the time Paris reached Aphrodite, goddess of love, he was learning the rules of the game. "What will *you* give me if I award the apple to you?" he said.

"What every mortal man wants most," she murmured, puckering her fulsome lips. "The love of the loveliest woman on Earth."

Paris did not hesitate. He laid the apple in Aphrodite's lap . . . then ran for his life as sandals and spears came flying after him.

So Aphrodite won the apple, and she was true to her word. She gave Paris the love of the most lovely woman on Earth: Helen. There was something she failed to mention, however: Helen was already married.

But then, that was Zeus's plan. When fair Helen laid eyes on Paris, she fell in love instantly and completely. Her husband was forgotten. All questions of right and wrong dissolved as she fled across the sea to the home of her handsome prince. As she fled to Troy.

In his rage and grief, her husband called on the King of Greece for help. The King called on his friends and allies to join forces with him and go after Helen–to make Paris and Troy pay for stealing her away. An army of thousands mustered their fleets of fast black ships, and prayed to the gods for success.

Now the gods, too, took sides.

"Oh, yes," said vengeful Hera, "I'll help defeat Paris."

"No," said Aphrodite, "Paris must have his Helen. I'm for Troy."

"So am I!" said Apollo. "There's a princess in Troy I'm particularly fond of."

"Well, I shan't rest till Troy is in ruins and the Trojans facedown in the

sea," said surly Poseidon. "I asked them for wages for building their precious walls. They told me they had a war to pay for, no money to spare. I'll make them pay for that."

For Athena the choice was harder. Troy, like Athens, was dedicated to her—its greatest treasure was a statue of her that the Trojans called the Luck of Troy. And yet Paris must pay. . . .

All the mortal world took sides in the Wars of Troy. And above them the gods, too, ranged themselves for or against the Trojans or the Greeks.

Zeus looked down from his seat of power and watched the earth bristle with columns of marching men. The nights twinkled with the fires of blacksmiths forging weapons. Shiploads of horses rode on the high seas.

It was his chessboard, all set up for the Great Game. With the unwitting help of the gods, the Wars of Troy would go on for years, killing men by the hundred, by the tens of hundreds—and women and children, too. The earth would be eased of the weight of human feet, the fields and woodlands left fallow. Everywhere would be washed clean in a tide of blood.

It was the perfect plan.

THE WOMAN NO ONE BELIEVED

APOLLO AND CASSANDRA

As well as the statue called the Luck of Troy, the Trojans had another treasure: Princess Cassandra. She was so beautiful, even as a child, that seven generals swore allegiance to the King of Troy, hoping to win her for a bride when she was older. She slept in a temple, so that no one would steal her away.

But it was Apollo's temple. When Apollo saw the sleeping Cassandra, what he saw roused more love in him than he had felt since his little friend Hyacinthus died. "Until you are a woman, Cassandra, and mine," he said. And he bent and kissed her little ears.

With his breath he passed her the gift of prophecy, so that when she woke Cassandra was even more of a marvel than before. For she could hear far-off voices talking of things to come. After the war broke out, the King and Queen would often ask her, "How will this end, Cassandra? How will this dreadful war end?" But the truth still lay far off, like a figure on a roadway still blurred by dust and distance.

When Cassandra was sixteen, in the middle of the war, Apollo came back to claim her. All swagger and bluster and arrogance, he swept into her room and said, "No more waiting! I have come for you!"

"I am honored, sir, but I've decided to stay unmarried."

"But, I'm Apollo the Shining! Apollo the Immortal! Look, here's my lyre!"

"Even so," said Cassandra. "Please go."

"But I love you! I gave you the gift of prophecy! I kissed your ears! I made you what you are today!"

Cassandra blushed. "Oh, was it you? I was asleep. You really should have woken me and asked if I *wanted* your gift. . . . You can take it back if you like."

Apollo was mortified. Never had his love and his presents been spurned so flatly. "A gift from the gods cannot be taken back," he complained. "Kiss me, at least!"

Cassandra supposed there would be no harm in that. So they kissed. And in his breath, Apollo passed to her a second gift, because he could not take away the first.

"Make your prophecies, Princess," he sneered, pushing her roughly away. "I have made you even more *gifted* than before."

When he had gone, into Cassandra's mind dawned a series of terrible visions: fires and blood, swords and a giant horse, ships and shadows and falling masonry. Her pretty face turned quite pale at the shock.

"Mother! Father! The Greeks are going to win! The Greeks are going to kill you and take me prisoner! I see it all!"

"Hush, hush, child. You don't look well. Lie down. You've had a nightmare. Troy is quite safe," said the King.

"*Troy will burn!*" yelled Cassandra, gripping his cloak. "*Don't you understand? I've seen it burning! Troy will burn!*"

But the wilder Cassandra became, the more the Trojans told themselves, "The Princess has gone mad. How tragic–such beauty tied to such madness." She was cursed, you see. Apollo had cursed her–with Disbelief.

Soon her dark hair was gray with frenzy, her beautiful face haggard and lined. She tore her clothes and ran through the streets seizing hold of passers-by. "The Greeks have a plan! They'll send a horse!" But no one believed her. No one. That was Apollo's revenge for his wounded pride.

After ten years of war, the Greeks built a horse–a great wooden horse, a tribute to Troy, the City of Horses. They left it on the beach, its wooden ears almost as high as the gated arch in Troy's wall. Then they sailed away, and all that was left were the black circles of a thousand campfires.

"*Burn it! Burn the horse! It's a trick!*" shrieked Cassandra. But by now she was only the ragged madwoman who ran about the streets with straws in her hair and desperation in her eyes.

With ships' hawsers they dragged the wooden horse in through the gates and stood it in the market square, dancing around it, celebrating their sudden and total victory.

"*Burn it! Destroy it!*" howled Cassandra. "*Can't you hear the soldiers' armor jingling inside? Can't you hear them breathing?*"

But Apollo's curse damned the Trojans as utterly as it had damned

Cassandra. They took no notice of her voice below their windows that night. They did not believe her when she said that the fast black ships were even now sailing back into the bay, that twenty Greek warriors were even now climbing down out of the wooden horse, unbarring the gate in the impenetrable wall, letting in the enemy to sack Troy.

It all happened just as she had seen it in her head. The towers fell in flames. The temples were looted. The King and Queen died. Cassandra was taken into slavery. And all the while, the giant wooden horse looked down with its painted eyes as if to say, "I believed you, Princess. I believed you all along."

"And Zeus's plan had worked out just as he had intended," said Hermes to Argus. "Countless men dead fighting over Troy. The race of Iron cut down to size. But then Zeus's plans always work. Zeus always has his way," Hermes added pointedly.

The monster to whom he said it shook its gigantic head. It might have been disagreeing—denying that Zeus would ever rescue Io from within her coily prison. Or it might simply have been shaking the buzzing flies from its ears, its nostrils, its hundred rheumy lashes.

A FREE MAN

HADES AND SISYPHUS

Princess Persephone spends half the year with her husband Hades in the gloomy Underworld, Land of the Dead. Spring and summer she spends with her mother Demeter in the sunshine, among the flowers and trees. But then she is a goddess. There is no such going to and fro for mortals.

Hades's kingdom is crowded and busy. Along its passageways, spirits stand in groups, debating:

". . . and I say, give me one firm spot to stand on, and . . ."

"Even so, nothing can come out of nothing, and nothing . . ."

"Yes, but, Pythagoras, what exactly *is* this hypotenuse?"

They do not talk of their families, the ones left behind in the sunshine, because on their boat journey from the Land of the Living they drank from the River Lethe and forgot all the joys of being alive. They are content. Hard to imagine, but true. Hades their king is not a jailer holding them prisoner under lock and key; it is simply

97

that they cannot leave. That is the Law of the Universe.

Once Odysseus, on his way home from the Wars of Troy, sailed to the Underworld to ask directions. Once a grieving widower came to beg for his wife back—almost succeeded, too. And once or twice, of course, people have tried to get out of dying. Take Sisyphus.

"Why should the gods live forever but not the likes of me?" groaned Sisyphus to his wife. He lay on his bed, green as a parrot, while Death hammered on the door. "They're not so clever, those gods on Olympus. They won't hold on to me. Do just as I tell you, Merope, and I'll be back, you see if I'm not!"

Snip! went the shears of Fate, and Sisyphus died.

After his soul embarked on its voyage along the River of the Underworld, his wife dumped his body behind a large rock in the garden, then put on her best red dress and invited the neighbors to a party.

"Never liked him! Glad he's gone!" she said, and drank a whole bottle of retsina toasting the boatman of Lethe.

"But, Merope dear, you adored him!" her bewildered neighbors began to say. But the widow quickly put her finger—"Shshsh!"—to her lips, and glanced at the sky.

"You see how she treats me?" raged Sisyphus, storming up and down the royal throne-room.

Hades sat on a throne of ebony whose blackness soaked up light like a sponge. Beside him, Persephone was a pool of autumnal reds and oranges, the flowers around her hair dried and brittle but lovely. "Poor man!" she said as she listened to Sisyphus's sorry story.

"No funeral! No pennies on my eyes! No tears! No dressing in widow's black! How can a man rest easy with a wife like that?"

Hades shook his head. He was deeply shocked at the behavior of Merope. It seemed the woman had given her husband no funeral rites at all! "She must be punished," he said grimly.

"She really should be," agreed Persephone.

"She ought to be punished!" exclaimed the spirits gathering by the door.

"Ah, well now, just imagine," said Sisyphus, "if you sent *me* to punish her. Wouldn't that give her the fright of her miserable life!"

Behind the rock in Merope's garden, Sisyphus's body rolled over as his soul reentered it. He got up, dusted himself off, shook the earth out of his hair, and sniffed deeply, savoring the sweet autumnal smoke of garden bonfires. Then he trotted back to the house and let himself in. "Home, dear!" he called.

Merope threw her arms around his neck. "You did it! You fooled them!"

"Didn't I say I would? 'Just let me go and punish her, then I'll come straight back,' I told them. That's what *they* think! Sisyphus die? It'll take more than Hades to put a stop to me!"

As he waited for Sisyphus to return to the Kingdom of the Dead, Hades

drummed his fingers on the arms of his ebony throne. "He said he would come straight back."

"Perhaps he can't find his wife to punish her," suggested Persephone.

"And perhaps he thinks he can trick me," growled Hades. "If he does, he will live to be very, very sorry."

Soon it was plain Sisyphus had no intention of coming back to Hades of his own accord. "He has taken a ship over my ocean," said Poseidon.

"He just passed by my forges at Etna," Hephaestus reported.

"He has built a little house on an island in the east," said Hestia, goddess of the hearth. "I smelled the smoke from his stove."

"He is growing old," said Athena, watching from the terraces of the Cloudy Citadel.

"There, see, in his hammock under the vine," said Zeus.

"Shall I fetch him *now?*" asked Death.

Once again Sisyphus entered the Kingdom of the Underworld. He hoped his trick had been forgotten. So many years had passed that he had almost forgotten it himself. But years are like days in the eyes of the gods, and their memories are long.

"Ah, Sisyphus! I have been waiting for you," said Hades, smiling at the ghostly wraith floating before his throne. "I have a little task for you." And he pointed to a large black boulder at the foot of a high, black hill. "When you have pushed the boulder to the top of that hill, Sisyphus, you may leave here. Yes, leave here forever."

So Sisyphus leaned his ghostly shoulder to the rock and started to push.

He was old now, and weary, but he pushed till the veins stood out on his brow, and his hands bled, and somehow he rolled the boulder a few inches up the hill. In a week he had reached halfway. In a month he was almost at the top. . . .

But then the rock slipped out of his grasp and rolled back down—all the way down to the bottom.

Do you hear that? No, it's not thunder. It is Sisyphus's rock rolling back down the hill for the thirty-seven-thousandth time. It will always be the same. Hades had decreed it as Sisyphus's punishment for defying the Law of the Universe.

And yet Sisyphus never gives up. Even as the rock bounces and thuds down the black hill, he mops his face with the rags of his clothes, and starts down behind it. "Next time," he says. "Next time I shall do it. And then I shall leave this place forever. A free man."

THE EYES OF ARGUS

THE BIRTH OF THE PEACOCK

"Have you heard the story before?" Hermes asked Argus, because the monster neither laughed nor wept to hear Sisyphus's fate. Then Hermes realized why. From end to end, Argus was fast asleep, its hundred lids shut, its flank rising and falling in slow, steady breaths.

Hera looked down out of Heaven and saw Hermes's raised sword.

"Argus, wake up!" called Hera.

But she was too late. The great tail uncurled: The little white calf trotted free, and the monster rolled onto its back and died.

"At last!" said Zeus with eager satisfaction.

But Hera cupped her two hands together and blew into them. When she opened her fists, a vicious gadfly went whirring earthward with the speed of a dart. It dived directly at Io the calf, buzzed in her flickering ears, and stung her little white rump. Io let out a bellow and began to run—along the beach, over the sand dunes, inland across the meadows, with the gadfly tormenting her every step of the way.

Meanwhile, Hera threw more magic, like a handful of gems, over the dying Argus. And when Hermes looked around, he gasped with amazement. There, rattling its fanlike, quivering tail, stood a bird whose every feather was tipped with an iridescent eye of green, purple, and blue. The world's first peacock lifted one foot, then the other, in a stately dance. Its cry was as shrill as a cry for help.

Help! Help!

But the peacock had no call to fear the sword of Hermes: It was far too beautiful a creature to kill.

The little white calf, on the other hand, was chased by the gadfly all the way to Egypt. Seeing her go, Zeus shrugged his shining shoulder and looked about him for another pretty face.

In Egypt Io ran through desert sand and desert cities, through souks crowded with dark faces and white robes. These people had seen camels, seen bony, gangling cattle, but never had they seen a creature as pretty as Io. And when she recovered her human shape and spoke—of being loved by a god and guarded by a monster and chased by a gadfly all the way to Egypt, they crowned her with rare desert flowers and brought her the water of holy pools and bowed down and worshiped her—first Queen of Egypt.

Listen. Is that thunder?

Yes. Dark clouds are gathering around the Cloudy Citadel. Other gods on other continents are colonizing the skies—African gods with black faces, Norse gods in a palace beyond the rainbow, a shipload of Egyptian gods with the heads of animals, Celtic gods who walk on the earth among mortal men.

But the snow still does not melt on the peak of Mount Olympus. And the stories are still being told, if not by Hermes, then by some other messenger.

And the peacock's hundred glistening, listening, feather-lashed eyes never, never close.

A GUIDE TO THE NAMES IN GREEK MYTHOLOGY

The pronunciation appears in parenthesis. Emphasize the part in *italics*.

ACTAEON (Ak-*tigh*-on) A huntsman who spied on Artemis and her handmaids while they were bathing.

APHRODITE (Af-roh-*digh*-tee) The goddess of love, sprung fully grown from the sea's frothy foam.

APOLLO (Ap-*oll*-oh) The son of Zeus and brother of Artemis, he was often thought of as the sun god, and therefore as important and powerful as Zeus himself; also the patron-god of music, archery, sports, and prophecy.

ARCAS (*Ar*-kas) Huntsman son of Callisto, with whom he was turned into a bear.

ARES (*Air*-ees) Bringer of War; immortal son of Zeus and Hera.

ARGUS (*Ar*-gus) Named in full, Argus Panoptes, or All-Seeing Argus, this giant or monster was created by Hera to keep watch with one hundred wakeful eyes.

ARTEMIS (*Ar*-te-miss) (or Diana) Goddess of the Moon, of hunting and of fertility, she was worshiped mostly by women.

ATHENA (Ath-*ee*-na) (or Pallas Athena) Only the most highly cultured civilization would boast such a goddess: patron of arts and handicrafts, wisdom and the olive tree; guardian of Athens.

CALLISTO (Ka-*list*-oh) Mother of Arcas: Great Bear in the night sky.

CASSANDRA (Kas-*sand*-ra) A mortal sweetheart of Apollo, to whom he gave the power of prophecy.

CECROPS (*Ke*-krops) First King of Attica (Greece), credited with building Athens, instituting marriage, and teaching proper worship of the Gods.

CELEUS (*Kel*-ee-us) King of Eleusis, visited by Demeter as she searched the world for her stolen daughter.

CENTAURS (*Sen*-tors) A mythical race, half-man, half-horse (probably originally men of Thessaly glimpsed hunting on horseback).

CEYX (*Kay*-ux) A mortal soldier, drowned at sea.

CLYMENE (*Kli*-me-nee) Doting mother of Phaeton and wife of Helios.

CLYTIE (*Kli*-tee-a) A sea nymph hopelessly in love with Apollo, who was changed into a flower.

CRONOS (*Kron*-oss) Youngest of the Titans, he fathered many of the Olympian gods. The Romans called him Saturn.

CYCLOPES (*Sigh*-klo-pees) Laborers in the volcanic workshops of Hephaestus the immortal blacksmith.

DEMETER (De-*mee*-ter) Goddess of the earth and of fruitfulness.

DEMO (*Dee*-moh) (properly) Demophon, Prince of Eleusis, almost rendered immortal by Demeter, but snatched back from the flames by his frightened mother.

DIONYSUS (*Digh*-o-*nigh*-sus) Thought of as god of wine, he was in fact god of "changed states" and could change shape himself as well as transforming mortals or driving them mad.

DRYADS (*drigh*-ads) Wood nymphs.

ERIS (*E*-riss) God of strife, he began the gods quarreling and indirectly caused the Trojan War.

EUROPA (Ure-*oh*-pa) Lovely mortal maiden carried off by Zeus who was disguised as a bull.

HADES (*Hay*-dees) Referred to as Pluto (because his true name was too terrible to say), he ruled the Underworld.

HALCYONE (Hal-*sigh*-on-ee) Immortal daughter of the West Wind, she chose to live as a seabird sooner than outlive her mortal husband.

HELEN (*Hell*-en) Fabulously beautiful princess abducted by Prince Paris of Troy, so starting the Trojan War.

HELIOS (*Hee*-lee-os) Driver of the chariot sun.

HEPHAESTUS (He-*figh*-stus) Ugly and deformed blacksmith god on whom the gods depended for weapons, armor, palaces. He even succeeded in marrying the goddess of love.

HERA (*Heer*-a) The Roman Juno, Hera was both sister and wife of Zeus, patron-goddess of marriage and childbirth, and is often pictured alongside a peacock.

HERMES (*Her*-mees) Mischievous errand boy to the gods, Hermes also escorted the Dead down to the Underworld, invented the alphabet, astronomy, measurement, and was the patron god of music, gymnastics . . . and thieves.

HESTIA (*Hess*-tee-a) Goddess of the hearth.

HYACINTHUS (High-a-*sinth*-us) Exquisitely handsome youth loved by Apollo.

IO (*Igh*-oh) Loved by Zeus, she was changed into a white calf, to protect her from Hera's jealousy.

LETO (*Lee*-toh) The Titan mother of Apollo and Artemis.

MAIA (*Migh*-a) Eldest of the seven Pleiades sisters and mother of Hermes.

MEROPE (*Mer*-o-pee) Wife of Sisyphus, who helped him try to cheat Death.

METANIRA (Met-an-*ire*-a) Queen of Eleusis, who deprived her son of immortality.

METIS (*Mee*-tiss) Zeus's first wife, whom he swallowed for fear of her giving birth to a son greater than he.

MUSES (*Mew*-zes) The three (sometimes nine) goddesses credited with inspiring in mortals poetry, music, drama, art, and invention.

NAIADS (*nigh*-ads) Freshwater nymphs from rivers, pools, or springs.

NEREIDS (*neer*-ee-ids) Sea nymphs of the Mediterranean.

ODYSSEUS (O-*diss*-ee-us) Mortal hero of the Trojan War, whose twenty-year voyage home was packed with adventures.

PARIS (*Pa*-riss) Prince of Troy, chosen by Zeus to judge the most beautiful goddess and fatally rewarded with the love of "the most beautiful woman on earth"–Helen.

PERSEPHONE (Per-*sef*-on-ee) Daughter of Demeter and bride, for half the year, of Hades, ruler of the Underworld.

PHAETON (*Figh*-ton) Half-mortal son of Helios, who drove his father's fiery chariot with disastrous results.

POSEIDON (Po-*sigh*-don) God of the seas.

RHEA (*Ree*-a) A very ancient Earth goddess, mother of Demeter, Hera, Hades, Poseidon . . . and Zeus.

SATYRS (*sat*-ers) Wild, disorderly followers of Dionysus, with bristly hair and snouty noses.

SEMELE (*Se*-me-lee) A mortal lover of Zeus who died on seeing him in his true divine glory, undisguised.

SISYPHUS (*Si*-si-fus) Odysseus's grandfather: A man so cunning that he thought he could even cheat Death.

TALOS (*Tal*-os) A giant brass man forged by Hephaestus.

TITANS (*Tie*-tans) The twelve sons and daughters of Heaven and Earth, ruling the world before the Olympians.

TYPHON (*Tigh*-fon) A terrible monster who fought Zeus for the conquest of the earth.

ZEPHYRUS (*Ze*-fer-us) The West Wind given shape as a god.

ZEUS (Zeuce, as in deuce) King of the Olympian gods, descended from the Titans and father of many gods and demigods; a lover of pretty women.